For Sara and my mother

First published 1991 by
Walker Books Ltd, 87 Vauxhall Walk
London SE11 5HJ

© 1991 Kim Lewis

Reprinted 1991, 1993
Printed and bound in Hong Kong by
South China Printing Co. (1988) Ltd

British Library Cataloguing in Publication Data
A catalogue record for this book is
available from the British Library.
ISBN 0-7445-1906-3

Emma's Lamb

Kim Lewis

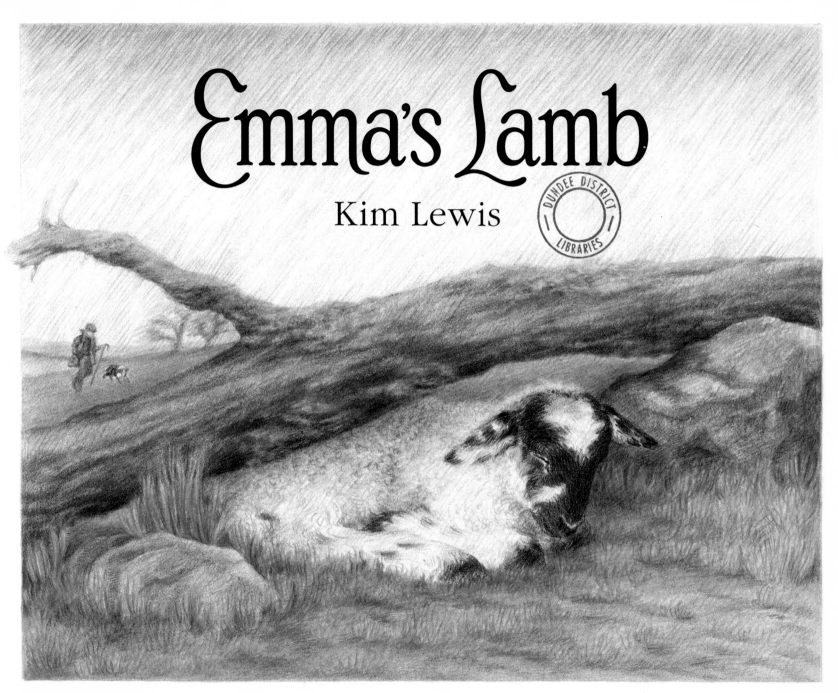

WALKER BOOKS LONDON

One rainy spring morning at lambing time,
Emma's father put a little lost lamb in a box
by the stove. Then he went back
to the field to look for Lamb's mother.

Lamb and Emma looked at each other.

"Baaa," said Lamb, sitting up in his box.

Emma wanted to keep little Lamb
and look after him all by herself.

So Emma dried Lamb

because he was very wet.

She tried to keep him warm

because he was very cold.

Emma fed Lamb

because he was very hungry.

When Lamb was dry and warm and fed,

he and Emma played.

"Baaa," said Lamb, getting

into a mess.

Then Emma took Lamb for a walk
and he skipped along behind her.
Emma decided to play hide and seek.
She closed her eyes and counted to ten.
"Here I come!" she cried.

Emma looked for Lamb in the stable.

She looked for him in the barn.

She looked for him in the granary.

She looked all around the yard.

She couldn't find Lamb in the house.

He wasn't in his box.

She couldn't find him in the

sheep pens either.

"I give up!" she shouted.

But Lamb was nowhere to be found.

Emma didn't want to play any more.

She wanted Lamb to come back.

She thought he might be cold and hungry.

"Where are you, Lamb?" she cried.

"Baaa," came a sound from the hayshed.

Emma ran inside to look.

Lamb sat up in the nesting box,

where the hens had laid their eggs.

"Baaa," he cried and ran to Emma.

"Lamb, I thought I'd lost you," said Emma,

holding him very tight.

She couldn't look after Lamb all by herself.

He needed to be with his mother.

But where was she?

Then Emma saw her father across the field.

A ewe without a lamb ran ahead of him, calling.

"Baaa," cried Lamb. He wriggled to get free.

Emma put him down,

and Lamb ran as fast as he could to his mother.

Emma went to the field the very next day.

When she called, Lamb came running to see her.

"Will you remember me?" asked Emma.

Lamb and Emma looked at each other.

"Baaa," said Lamb, waggling his tail.